For: Simon & Gracie

If Dashiel can do...

So can you

Merry Christmas

12/8/12

Santa Stories

The True Tale of Dasher

Written by Alan Jania

Illustrated by Cami Woodruff

For information on bulk sales, contact:
Dasher the Dependable Reindeer, LLC
3010 Royal Queens Court
St. Charles, IL 60174
(630) 513-7737
www.dasherchristmas.com

Printed in the United States by Evangel Press, Nappanee, Indiana

ISBN 978-0-9885857-0-6

Written by: Alan Jania
Illustrated by: Cami Woodruff

Story Editors: Carmelita Linden, Marlene Targ Brill

Art Direction, Design & Production:
Christina Canright, Canright Communications

Dedication

We dedicate this story to Gregory Falduto, Leo Henning and Walter Jania, and their dependable comrades, both men and women, who served our country in World War II, the Korean Conflict, Vietnam War, Operation Desert Storm and the Iraq War.

They brought us all of the Christmas joy we have engaged in during the past 67 years, and their heroics will never be forgotten. The American "Can Do" attitude lives on in their children, grandchildren and great grandchildren.   – Dasher

FROM HIS TOP-FLOOR WINDOW, Santa Claus looked out over all of Christmas Town. Snowflakes glistened off tree branches, danced in the glow of the streetlights and laid a shiny white cover on the toy factory roofs. Inside, the buildings glowed with activity as elves bustled to make all the toys on Santa's list.

Santa puffed out his chest with pride. "The North Pole may be a cold and blustery place," Santa thought. "But the magic of Christmas Town is its Christmas spirit that makes it feel toasty year 'round with good cheer."

Santa settled into his favorite comfy chair, a mug of hot cocoa warming his hands. The fire in the fireplace blazed and crackled. He watched as Mrs. Claus made sure each little reindeer was neatly tucked in warm and cozy, and ready for the nightly bedtime story.

"Which story shall I tell the reindeer children tonight?" Santa wondered. He thought of the many special Christmas Eves he spent with his elite sleigh teams. "How about that foggy Christmas Eve saved by a red-nosed

reindeer?" His mind wandered even further back, to one of his favorite and most dependable reindeer. That's it. "This is a tale about a Christmas that almost didn't happen," Santa began.

Eyes widened as the reindeer children now wanted to hear more.

Deep in the forest on a cold and snowy night just like tonight, a fawn was born, and his parents named him Dasher. Like all Christmas Town reindeer parents, Dasher's parents dreamed that some day their buck would fly with my Christmas Sleigh Team.

At the age of four, all reindeer in Christmas Town attend Leaping, Flying & Landing Reindeer Academy—in a year or two each of you will be in class. The Academy trains the best of the best to lead my sleigh on Christmas Eve. We begin with the most dedicated reindeer in class. They train alongside that year's reindeer team who are busily preparing for the Christmas Eve ride.

The year that Dasher began at the Reindeer Academy we had an especially promising group of young reindeer. The students knew Dasher as one of the fastest in the forest. Donner, Blitzen, Comet and Vixen were strong and could leap the highest. Little Cupid could land right where he needed to, while Dancer's hooves could cling to the iciest of roofs. And, gentle Prancer was so delicate it was certain he'd never wake a child sleeping below.

At that time, Nickoly was my trusted Master Trainer and Captain of the reindeer team. Every day he would watch the student reindeer at recess, and he noticed that young Dasher always made sure that all the reindeer were included in hoofball games. Even the smallest fawn got a chance to play. In fact, Nickoly was the first to see "There was something extra special about that Dasher!" He had what Nickoly called a "can do" spirit.

Winter set in at the North Pole and the winds grew strong and the nights icy cold. But Christmas Town was warm in the glow of lights that

shone from every building. Elves worked their magic day and night, making the toys and wrapping them for Christmas Eve delivery.

Everything was going on schedule, until four weeks before Christmas. Suddenly and unexpectedly, the Polar Flu hit! One by one, my elite reindeer sleigh team took sick, so sick they couldn't get up from their beds, and they certainly were in no shape to fly. When Christmas Town's doctor arrived at the barn, he had even worse news: The flu medicine would take weeks to cure everyone.

I left the barn with Nickoly at my side. Sick, and now worried, he asked, "What will happen if we can't fly?"

Sadly I answered, "There will be no Christmas."

Word had traveled fast through Christmas Town...No Christmas for the world's children?

Each night after taking his medicine, Dasher would close his eyes and try to sleep, but all he could think about was Christmas. He tossed and turned all night.

A few days later, Dasher woke up and felt better. His head didn't ache. Dasher climbed out of bed and realized he was no longer sick! He heard voices outside, and saw some of his friends playing in the snow. It seemed the medicine had worked wonders on the younger reindeer and most had recovered already.

The next morning, before anyone awoke, Dasher walked to the sleigh barn just as he had done many mornings before. But this morning was sadly different: The bright shiny sleigh would not fly this Christmas Eve. Tears in his eyes, Dasher thought of all the disappointed children. He wondered out loud, "Is there something I can do?" Then, the idea came to him in a flash.

Filled with excitement, Dasher called together all the young reindeer from the Academy. They met in the farther reaches of the forest. The young reindeer huddled around Dasher. "We've been watching and practicing alongside this year's Sleigh Team reindeer for months, right? Well then,

why can't we put together a sleigh team of our own? We might be the youngest reindeer at the Academy, but we are the only ones who can help Santa! Children need Christmas! We can't let them down, can we?"

"No!" they cheered. Being young and small wasn't going to hold back this team of reindeer!

True to their word, they immediately got started. Night after night, they gathered in the forest clearing and practiced their sleigh team moves until dawn. They kept improving, but with only a week to go, Dasher feared not fast enough.

Hoping a walk in the forest would make him feel better, Nickoly came across the hard-working young reindeer. "What are you all doing here?" Nickoly asked, with concern. Dasher explained, "This year's sleigh team is still very sick, and Christmas Eve is only a few days away. I know we're the youngest class at the Academy, but we have been working very hard. We can do the Christmas Eve flight with Santa." Nickoly walked around the makeshift practice area and watched as each young reindeer jumped, leapt and flew through the air.

Dasher said to Nickoly, "We are all very excited about helping Santa. We want to make the children happy around the world. But now I am a little worried…what if we have not practiced enough? What if something goes wrong? What if we get Santa lost? Do YOU think we really can do this?"

Nickoly told me later that all the young reindeer stopped what they were doing to hear what he had to say: "You need to train and plan as much as you possibly can. I am feeling a bit better now, so I can help you with that."

But it isn't just the reindeers' skill that gets Santa and his sleigh around the world," he added. "Each reindeer has to know how important he or she is to the team and believe in the magical spirit of Christmas. This spirit will fuel the elite team of reindeer. It's this spirit that lets them soar through the sky and deliver the presents in just one night. Find this magical spirit, and your team can do it all," said Nickoly. Everyone cheered and went back to training with even more enthusiasm than before.

Nickoly took Dasher aside and said softly, "I can see this spirit in you. We have a few days left. With lots of hard work and believing in that spirit,

I know Santa will have his sleigh team for Christmas Eve!" Dasher felt his old "can do" feeling return. If Nickoly had confidence in him, he could have confidence too!

They had no time to lose. Nickoly, still weak from the Polar Flu, but filled with pride, leapt into action. As the days went by, Nickoly worked with Dasher on the all-important sleigh team positions. "You need to have the right reindeer in the right place," he said. They considered the strengths of each of fawn and doe, and assigned them to the position where they would most be needed.

Nickoly knew just the thought of canceling Christmas made me heartsick. All of Christmas Town kept hoping for some sort of Christmas miracle. What Dasher didn't know was that as the team was getting better and better, Nickoly came to me daily with his report. Now it was just three days to Christmas Eve. Each day Nickoly had convinced me to wait.

At first when he told me what Dasher and the young reindeer had been up to, I laughed, thinking how very sweet. But Nickoly was not laughing...

Had anyone else told me of such a daring plan, I'd have stopped it right there. Christmas Eve landings are not like the school practice rooftops, they can be dangerous. I'd not risk our young reindeer, even to save Christmas. But Nickoly held firm, and I have always trusted Nickoly's advice.

With just two days left before Christmas Eve, Nickoly asked me to meet him in front of the sleigh barn to see Dasher's team in action. Sensing something was about to happen, all of Christmas Town was out waiting to see if Christmas would indeed be canceled.

A hush swept over the crowd as I stepped in front of the sleigh barn. The big doors slid open, and out of the dark interior came the young reindeer, with Dasher leading the way. They were all wearing the Christmas harnesses. Two by two, they came with bells jingling as they pranced out pulling my sleigh to the wonder of the crowd. The reindeer team looked proud and magnificent. As sick as their parents were, they were anxious but also bursting with pride as I stepped up and took my seat in the sleigh.

With a snap of the reins, the sleigh lifted as smoothly as I can ever remember. We climbed high up above the crowd. The team of reindeer had never flown so high, and I could see all of Christmas Town, which looked like a toy village from so far above. We circled twice and touched back down as gently as snowflakes fall in the woods. The crowd erupted with cheers and whistles. They all knew that Christmas was saved! A team of reindeer who truly understood the spirit of the Christmas season would save Christmas.

By now the glow of the fireplace was almost out... Santa looked at the young reindeer around him in the room. "I was so proud of Dasher that day." Santa told them. "Dasher believed that he and the young reindeer could do something to make a difference, and Nickoly helped Dasher believe. It was Dasher's 'can do' spirit that saved Christmas that year."

"From history class at the Leaping, Flying & Landing Reindeer Academy, you know that, like Nickoly, Dasher went on to serve as Captain of

my reindeer team for many years. And, like Nickoly, I knew I could always depend on Dasher."

The embers remained glowing in the fireplace, but the fawns, some half asleep, were ready for bed. "Sleep well and sweet dreams of leading my sleigh."

And me? I settle back into my chair and ask the same question I ask myself every year. Softly, I say out loud, to no one in particular. "Who can do the task this year? Who can lead my sleigh team?"

Around the doorframe a little head appeared. One of the young fawns tilted his head, wiped some of the sleep from his eyes and looked at me with a sly little smile and said, "I can do!"

I'll have to keep my eye on THAT one!